Last Performance at the Three Dragons Inn

Novelette: The Song of the Burning Heart

I0532966

Ben Spencer

Copyright © 2024 by Ben Spencer

All Rights Reserved

Cover Design by Doyle Hinkle

This is a work of fiction. Names, incidents, and characters are either the product of the author's imagination or are used fictitiously. Any resemblance to persons living or dead, or locales, is entirely coincidental.

ISBN-13: 9781732038059

KNOCK-KNEE BOOKS

A Note from the Author

If you are reading this, it's likely that you have already subscribed to my newsletter over at benspencer.substack.com. If you haven't subscribed, I hope that you will consider doing so. Updates on *The Song of the Burning Heart* series can be found on the newsletter.

Last Performance at the Three Dragons Inn is a novelette set a little more than one-hundred-and-fifty years prior to the events of my forthcoming epic fantasy novel, *The Prophecy of the Yubriy Tree*. The characters and the events in *Last Performance at the Three Dragons Inn* are referenced in *The Prophecy of the Yubriy Tree*, in a manner that makes clear that very few people, if any, know the truth of what took place. This, then, is the true story of what happened in Low Osgood all those years ago.

Jezebel thought it strange to perform in front of an amphitheater only half-full, and stranger yet to perform in front of those who couldn't afford the price of admission. The audience was composed of common locals, not the customary purse-plenty tourists: Briar and Biff, oversized twin bakers from the village, sat stage left, chins in their hands like a pair of attentive gargoyles; while down front, Tabitha the seamstress sat suckling her babe, gazing raptly at the players.

Jezebel noted these and more, though when she looked at the crowd, her attention was drawn mostly to the proprietor of the Three Dragons Inn—Shayla Long-Eyes. Shayla was planted in the center-front of the amphitheater, where she sat like the sun, orbited by an inner ring of empty benches. The outer rows were spotted with the lucky invitees, the first theater-goers in history to watch a performance of *The Flame* without relinquishing the coin to spend a night in the inn.

"It's fortunate for us that our shit performance is lost on this lot, but you better believe our Lady of the Long Eyes has made note of it," Meric whispered to Jezebel backstage as they prepared for the play's climactic scene.

Jezebel nodded but didn't reply. She was too busy trying to mount a dragon. Meric, Theon and Osten merely had to push the props, but Jezebel had an eight-step ascent in the dark to the bridge of the dragon Teriquay's emerald-green neck. Add to the fact that she was dressed in a sheer lace slip after spending the previous hour and a half performing in the coarsest roughspun, and her quietude was understandable.

"Hush!" Osten mocked Meric from across the way. "Our butterfly doesn't differentiate between queen and commoner! Her wings must shine, regardless of who sees!"

Jezebel closed her eyes, ignoring the actors' prattle. Positioned now, she leaned forward and wrapped her arms around Teriquay's neck, searching with her hands until she found the grips notched in the wood. Behind her, the men readied themselves at the dragons' wheels, ready to push the trio on stage. She had heard the dragons praised as the greatest stage props in all of Ragar Or—greater even than those used by the Swans, Union's own acting company. Jezebel believed it. With her eyes closed, Jezebel felt that she was astride Teriquay herself: every night when the curtains opened and King Reuel's boat appeared before her, Jezebel was filled with the same power the dragonfeeder must have experienced near four decades before, when she descended from the heavens and laid waste to nearly the entire Salk dynasty.

The side curtains opened, revealing two of the legendary beasts to the crowd. The crowd oohed and aahed, though Jezebel well knew that the audience was saving their biggest reaction for Teriquay.

"Look, Father!" Prince Daeguss shouted from the ship once the crowd had settled. "It's the blue dragon...Comet! And over there, all brown and white...Mooncalf!"

Meric and Osten rolled the dragons out toward the stationary boat in the center of the stage where King Reuel and his wife and children blithely awaited their fate. In reality, all four of the king's children had been on board, but this being a play, one precocious youngster sufficed for the entire brood. The prince sounded horribly stupid shouting the dragons' names like they were trained dogs, but Jezebel knew that was only the case in retrospect: there had been no reason at the time for the young princeling to believe the dragons were anything but tame. Comet and Mooncalf had long been known as peaceful creatures that loved to fly above the boats on Lake Wyglass. It was why the king had traveled north to Low Osgood, and why his family was with him. The Salks had come to see the dragons, the ones that, in this glorious age of unification, performed for man.

On stage, the actor playing King Reuel sounded Jezebel's cue. "They are a pair, which means they are blessed by the Twins, and they are creatures of the air, which delights Stavus. The gods shine on these creatures, just as the gods shine on all of Ragar Or."

The curtain pulled back, and Jezebel was exposed. The commoners in the crowd shrieked and gasped at the sight of the wooden green dragon, knowing what was coming. Jezebel, whose speaking part for the evening was finished, acted with her eyes; she gazed down from Teriquay's neck at the doomed king and his family with a burning intensity, underscoring her transition from ill-treated peasant girl to sorceress of the air. She knew that the audience would take in the dragon first, but then their eyes would go to her, and she didn't intend to disappoint. The blue-painted whorl on Jezebel's cheek dazzled, a vibrant cosmos. It had been touched up and enlarged backstage. *The telling mark,* they called it—the sign of the Jeyedoshi. Although Jezebel doubted that the actual dragonfeeder's whorl had been quite so flamboyant.

"Father," the princeling said as Jezebel and Teriquay approached, "look. It's the green dragon. The wild one."

Theon, crouched low to minimize his exposure, rolled the wooden dragon forward with an ominous slowness. Jezebel was close friends with a Low Osgood old-timer who had been lakeside that day. He said Teriquay had floated down from a nearby mountain like a bird of prey sizing up an injured meal. There had been no rush, no hurry, only the elegantly menacing beating of the dragon's wings.

"Teriquay," King Reuel declared. "She's wild, yes, but as harmless as the other two." The actor put an arm around his son. He wore an uneasy smile. "She must have sensed that we were here. She's come to pay homage."

Brionne, Reuel's queen, was given the honor of the last words. "Reuel," she said, grabbing at her husband's arm. "Look! Teriquay has a rider. Why does she have a rider?"

The play came to a deliberate standstill. The wooden dragons stopped moving, while on the boat the royal family stood motionless, holding on to one another. For two full seconds no one moved. Then, in a rush, Theon pushed Teriquay forward, to within inches of the boat. The Salk family shrieked and shielded their faces from an imaginary flame.

Out in the audience, a traumatized quiet took hold. The actors held themselves still as statues as stagehands covered in black tunics and black breeches filed in from both sides of the stage, carrying torches. They formed a wall of flame that cordoned off the players, who slowly and quietly exited the stage. Jezebel didn't move: once shielded by the flame wall, Meric, Osten, and Theon moved to the front of the wooden dragons and rolled them back behind the curtain. Jezebel stayed stock still-throughout, remaining in character until she disappeared entirely from the audience's view.

*

Backstage there were bottles of blush wine and plates of exotic cheeses and chilled saucers loaded with crudo fresh from the Blackstar Isles. All in all, the standard post-production fare. The players had the morrow off, which normally would have been the occasion for a bit of excess, but the enormity of what beckoned two days hence was putting a hamper on the revelry. Osten kept trying to lighten the mood by crisscrossing the dressing room without wearing pants, while Angiel, the actress who played Queen Brionne, entertained with off-the-cuff impressions of the evening's audience. But the shallow spirit of their frivolity was made apparent the moment Shayla Long-Eyes appeared: Osten unceremoniously put away his cock and balls, and Angiel, caught in the middle of a rather bawdy and mean-spirited impersonation, turned prim as a Winged Woman, pursing her lips and crossing her legs and waiting, like everyone else, to hear what Shayla had to say.

"That was not a stellar performance," Shayla declared simply when all eyes were on her. There was no cut to her words, no anger, only the truth. She let her eyes roam the room, until they rested on Jezebel. "Jezebel being the exception."

Jezebel gave a slight curtsy. She willed herself not to look at Shayla's entourage, who had trailed into the room behind her. Donnell Tyne—Jezebel's onetime lover—numbered among them. Five years later, and it still stung to look at him. Donnell had been Jezebel's beau back when she first won the part of the dragonfeeder, but then Shayla—who was near twenty-six years Jezebel's senior—swooped in and stole Donnell from her with a brutal efficiency that still stunned after all this time. One day Jezebel was with Donnell, smiling at him beneath the sheets, and the next day Donnell was on Shayla's arm, with naught but curt, mean-spirited words for Jezebel when she begged for an explanation. "She gives all the new girls a taste of her power," one of the other actresses explained to Jezebel a few days later. "Learn your lesson, and let it go." Jezebel hadn't believed the actress back then, but she did now. She had seen too many similar examples since.

Osten offered Shayla an excuse. "The adoration of the common crowd was too easily won. We as a company are conditioned to expect a certain level of pretension from the audience. Without it...why, we have nothing to strive for onstage!"

Osten won himself a few chuckles. But most waited on Shayla's response before deciding if Osten's quips were indeed funny.

Shayla moved deeper into the room, claiming the space. Jezebel watched, wondering, as she often did, whether she looked as much like Shayla as the other players claimed. They shared the same dark blonde hair, the same oval face, and the same shapely cut; but when Jezebel looked at Shayla Long-Eyes, she didn't see an older version of herself. What she saw was a terrifying vastness. The older woman was in every way...more. Shayla Long-Eyes inhabited the world as if the gods had granted her a deed in their will.

"Osten, I'll allow that most of the villagers left the play happily unawares. But I was in the audience too. Did you fail to see me?" Shayla asked the question while looking at Osten, but at the end her gaze drifted, taking in the room.

No one answered. A few heads bobbed.

Shayla smiled. She wore a gown of green samite with intricate gold threadwork. The hem whispered against the stone as she made her way toward Osten. When she reached him, she took his chin in her hands. "The next time you perform, the queen of Ragar Or will be in attendance. Will she inspire you as I could not?"

Osten, usually so skilled with his tongue, struggled to string together a coherent run of words. "Shayla, no queen could…you are, above all…though of course I will, we will…"

Shayla closed her eyes. Dropped Osten's chin. Then she lifted her head and swept the room with her piercing, all-seeing gaze. The players waited with drawn breath, fearful of the woman's power. *She acts the queen,* Jezebel thought. *She wants to remind us of who she is, before the real queen enters the city.*

Shayla spoke, her voice cool and detached. "The night after next will be the most important night of your lives. You will perform in front of Queen Portia Salk, a woman who might, with a wave of her hand, end your life. There are even rumors that that's why she's come. Some say she's traveled to Low Osgood to have her revenge against a play that dares portray the Salk family without her leave. Once her curiosity is sated, she will execute all the performers and burn the Three Dragons Inn to the ground."

Jezebel shuddered. *It's only village talk,* she told herself. More prevalent was talk of the queen's excitement at seeing the play in person, word of *The Flame*'s popularity having spread far and wide.

Shayla donned a wicked grin. "Or not. Instead, we might be on the cusp of eternal fame, eternal wealth, eternal glory. The strength of our respective performances might alter the course of our lives. Perhaps even alter the course of a *queen's* life. But if we are to rise to the occasion, we must find within us that divine spark which compels us to greatness. When onstage, we must bring to life the death of the queen's dear departed family with a vividness that will shake Queen Portia to her very core. Only then will we truly honor her. Only then will we truly be worthy of whatever fate the rightful ruler of Ragar Or has in store for us."

The Long-Eyes sought out Jezebel once more. She stared at Jezebel with a brazen unselfconsciousness, as if the two of them were the only people in the room. Jezebel let her eyes go soft, but she met Shayla's stare all the same. She was long practiced in the art. The trick, she had learned, was to pretend that Shayla had your best interests at heart.

From across the room, Shayla smiled at Jezebel. Only at Jezebel. "In order to achieve this greatness, some of us must risk more than others. Some of us must blur the very line between performance and reality."

There is no line between performance and reality, Jezebel thought. It was a lesson she had learned long ago, long before she was ever introduced to Shayla Long-Eyes. It was a truth she held deep in her heart. For Jezebel, acting and living were of one piece. But, as always, Jezebel kept her thoughts to herself, and gave Shayla only soft eyes, signaling agreement.

Abruptly, it was over. Shayla Long-Eyes, confident that she had taken the measure of Jezebel's soul, broke off her gaze. "In two days then," she said to all. She left the room, her entourage trailing in her wake.

The other players waited until she was out of earshot before exhaling. As usual, it was Osten who broke the silence. "In two days," he declared soberly, holding a wine-filled cup aloft. "Let the good Queen Portia think of our play what she will. But let our lady of the Long-Eyes know beyond the shadow of a doubt that we left our lifeblood on the stage."

Everyone in the room raised their cups.

Jezebel included.

*

The sky was purple at dawn, the sun clotting behind Simstone Mountain. Upon awakening, Jezebel went to the eastern window and stared down at the amphitheater, now backlit by the rising sun. The Three Dragons Inn had been built into the side of Simstone; only when it was built it hadn't been the Three Dragons Inn, but instead the manse of an immensely powerful gorgostrine—a holy man of the Twins. It was common knowledge that, on the same spot where the amphitheater now stood, the gorgostrine had once conducted hundreds of twin-death rites: the old Ontish custom that paired adolescents together and forced them to fight to the death.

There were mornings when Jezebel's thoughts lingered on these past horrors, but not today. Today she tried to focus on her breathing. Once the day wound into gear, she knew it would be near impossible to settle into her body, so she wanted to touch base now: she went through a progression of short inhalations and long exhalations before settling into an even, rhythmic flow, four seconds breathing in, four seconds breathing out. At some point she closed her eyes. She opened them again when the color of the inside of her eyelids turned orange, the sun having topped Simstone.

Time to go. The queen would be arriving in Low Osgood shortly, and Jezebel wanted to reach her destination before the crowds packed the streets.

Outside of Jezebel's room, the long rosewood hallway was quiet. Mornings in the inn weren't normally noisy, but often there were a number of early risers among the affluent patrons who stayed there; it wasn't uncommon for Jezebel to find herself engaged in conversation with an admirer the moment she stepped out of the room. But not today. Save for the handful of actors and actresses who lived in The Three Dragons, the entire inn had been cleared in advance of Queen

Portia's arrival. By evening, every vacant room would be filled with members of the queen's traveling court. Queen Portia herself was expected to take up residence in the Inn's tower apartment.

Jezebel descended a spiral staircase, emerging onto a splash of cool black and white marble in the recently renovated foyer. She hurried out the large oaken doors, skipping her ritual glance back at the sculpted dragons watching from the roof. Even without looking, Jezebel could see Teriquay in her mind's eye, dominant in the center, roaring at all who approached.

The morning was crisp and cool. Jezebel walked briskly down the winding road that led to the Three Dragons Inn, unspooling into Low Osgood. A quarter mile ahead, the alluring form of Lake Wyglass glistened like a chimera, beckoning awestruck eyes to come and see if it was make-believe. The body of water rippled with silver and sunlight, looking less a geographic feature than a portal to dreams. It was the lake that made the Three Dragons Inn possible: the resort town had sprung up around Wyglass's beguiling charm, first tempting dragons, then royalty, and more recently the wealthy to come and visit. These days *The Flame* helped drive the affluent to Low Osgood, but the subject matter of the play was so inextricably linked to Wyglass that only a fool would believe that *The Flame* would have experienced similar success in a different city.

Veering west, Jezebel made her way into the beating heart of Low Osgood, the area the locals referred to as Lowlow, short for Lower Low Osgood. Here, the conditions became considerably more cramped, the smells considerably more ripe, and the sights considerably less refined. All three were in instant evidence as Jezebel pushed herself against the wall of a smithy to avoid a scowling codger driving a quartet of pigs up Black Street. Nearby, a woman made a peculiar song out of a string of obscenities, a large gray rat dashed from one gutter to another, and two boys played knockabout, taking turns boxing each other in the ears to see who would fall first.

Jezebel beat onward, unfazed. Leaving Black Street, Jezebel turned onto the Vanishing, the area where Black, Talc, and Guttergrow Streets intersected in quick order, forming a neat triangle of escape routes. The centerpiece locking the three streets was the highest hovel in all Lowlow, a wooden two-story shack of surprisingly sturdy construction. It was a home, of all things, the residence of the man chiefly responsible for shepherding Jezebel through adolescence after her father died.

Jezebel's father's best friend. Bal Whitewood.

Jezebel opened the door and slipped inside. The downstairs was dark, save for where the sun filtered through a stairway aperture. Jezebel hurried toward the light, knowing that was where Bal was waiting.

The back of Bal's bald head greeted Jezebel at the top of the stairs. He sat on a hard, wooden chair, looking out over the lake through the slats of a rotting porch railing.

"Tell me true, Jezzy," Bal said without turning around. "Do you think the queen will show her face when she's winding her way through the Serpent? It's not likely, is it? She'll be holed up inside her carriage, hidden away from the prying eyes of the likes of me."

Jezebel approached and gave Bal a chaste kiss on the back of his bald head. She followed Bal's gaze to the where the Serpent Road came into view, edging close to Wyglass. "She's said to be a friend to the common man. I think there's reason to hope that she'll show her face along the way. Though she'll be little more than a blur from here."

"A glimpse is all I want," Bal smacked through sandpaper lips. "You'd think my eyes would be sated from the first royal feast, but in my latter years I find that I hunger for a second. I saw her brother too, you know."

"You saw her brother burnt on the lake. King Reuel and his wife and children."

Bal nodded vigorously. "That I did. Burnt by the green one, the sly one. The dragonfeeder whispered in

Teriquay's ear and down from the mountaintop she came, eager to kill a king."

Jezebel took a seat beside Bal in the wooden chair's twin. A sweet caress of wind rose above the stench in the streets and played at her dark blonde hair. "I play the part of the dragonfeeder in the play. Over at the Three Dragons Inn."

Bal's chin labored up and down, but, as Jezebel expected, he avoided the matter of her vocation upon resuming the conversation, choosing instead to revert to his memories of the past. "Your father couldn't believe it when I told him what had happened. Tanners we were, at Coffyn Castle. The king's dead, I said, him and his whole family burnt to a crisp."

Jezebel reached over and touched Bal on the arm. "My father loved you like a brother."

"That he did. And I him. I told him that I'd take care of you as he lay dying. And I kept that vow. I keep it to this day."

Their roles of who cared for who had long since reversed, not that Jezebel felt the need to point it out. Bal had taken care of her when it mattered. Back when she was young, and newly parentless. Back when the world was crashing in. Bal had stolen her away from Coffyn Castle when the lady of the castle had wanted her dead, relinquishing his place in the world in the process. And he had never once complained of the sacrifice, not even during the lean years when he had bounced between occupations, not even when he'd been forced to spend a stretch farming leeches. He was a rare sort, her Bal, the only man of his kind she'd ever encountered.

"You've done right by me, Bal. I'll never forget it."

They sat in silence for a moment, watching the shimmering, sun-kissed lake. Lowlow or not, it was still one of the best views in the city. Directing her attention toward the Serpent, Jezebel could see the first of the spectators lining the road, anticipating the queen's arrival.

"Queen Portia is coming to see the play," Jezebel said, treading once more into territory she knew Bal would rather avoid. She had never understood his reluctance to discuss her occupation, but she had respected it nevertheless, believing she owed him the favor of this one peculiar preference. But her impending performance in front of the queen weighed too heavily for Jezebel not to share her worries with the person she trusted most in the world. "She's going to be in the audience as I sit astride a great wooden dragon and pretend to burn her family to death. Even worse, she'll watch my transformation into the dragonfeeder. Bal, I know it's only a play, and I know that Queen Portia is renowned for her wisdom and kindness, but if ever there was a vengeful bone in the queen's body, who better to punish for her brother's death than the actress playing the dragonfeeder?"

Bal grimaced. Without seeming to be fully aware of what he was doing, he flicked his hand, as if shooing away Jezebel's words.

"Bal, I don't under—"

"This is the price a person pays for courting fame," Bal interrupted, giving the arm of the wooden chair a little slap. "I've tried to warn you, Jezzy. Live a small life. You of all people should know the dangers of bringing attention to yourself. It was years after we fled the castle before I got a good night's sleep. I worried constantly that the Lady Esme would find us, would find you—"

"The Lady Esme died less than six months after we fled. And it was her superstitions alone that made you worry for my life. The others, even Lord Coffyn, didn't share her beliefs. You said yourself that we could have returned to no ill harm—"

"And yet I kept us clear away, didn't I? Because what's your life to a lord who'd rather not worry that your presence is the cause of every bit of ill luck to pass his way? All I wanted for you was a chance to live your life without having to worry that you'd always be associated with being a lesser twin. I didn't want anyone to think you a...a...jeyedoshi. But now you play the part of the dragonfeeder, a jeyedoshi if there ever was one."

Ah. At last, Bal's reticence to discuss her acting career made sense.

"I'm no jeyedoshi, Bal. You know that. I have no telling mark. I don't speak to animals." She laughed as she said it, but even as she laughed, she remembered the day she had tried out for the role of the dragonfeeder, the words Shayla Long-Eyes had said to her the instant she finished her audition. *You were born to this role, little sister.* And then Shayla had selected her on the spot, sending away the other girls, true actresses all, flabbergasted and confused.

Bal turned in his chair and looked at her. She felt stripped bare by his gaze, his dark brown eyes burrowing into the very soul of her. He stared long and hard, before suddenly, as if coming back into himself, relenting. "My Jezzy," he said. "I'm an old man now. And you a woman grown. You've risen to such heights." He looked at her once more, but this time only at her clothes, a green linen tunic of a quality cut. She always dressed simply for her outings to the Lowlow, but even so, she couldn't hide what she'd become. "There's so little I can do for you. But as you said, you're no jeyedoshi. Play your part true, and, if Queen Portia is just, she will recognize you for who you truly are."

Jezebel didn't respond. She had no idea whether Bal had given her a blessing, or a curse.

*

Bal was old, but he was neither senile nor doddering, so once Jezebel had given him the gift of her time, she took her leave. She could see from the porch railing that the streets were beginning to fill. Later in the day she would see Queen Portia up close at the Three Dragons Inn, but that in no way tempered her desire to watch the royal procession enter the city.

She knew a place close to the water where she would have a decent view. She decided to go there at once. But when she stepped outside Bal's front door, Shayla Long-Eyes was waiting for her.

For a moment Shayla said nothing, instead allowing the shock of her appearance to settle in Jezebel's bones. The Long-Eyes had coiled irises of deep blue that verged on purple, and when she looked at people, she gave the impression that she was communing with their thoughts. Jezebel felt instantly guilty, forgetting that she had nothing to feel guilty about. It took her a moment to realize that it wasn't guilt she felt but fear: Shayla had peeled back a layer of Jezebel's private life, and now Jezebel had one less place to hide from the Long-Eyes's gaze.

"The dragonfeeder lived on Guttergrow when she was a child. Have you visited the place?"

Jezebel was thrown by Shayla's decision to ask a question in lieu of a greeting, but she quickly recovered.

"Yes. I've been there. The alehouse."

"The Spider Hole, they call it, though at the time it was stupidly called The Drunkard. Would you accompany me there?"

Jezebel was flummoxed. She supposed that was Shayla's intention. "I had hoped to see Queen Portia enter the city."

Shayla gave her a thin, well-practiced smile. It was the smile of a woman who wouldn't take no for an answer. "You will see the queen later, will you not? And from a better vantage point than most. Come with me. What I have to show you will not keep." She turned and walked away without waiting for a reply, heading shortly down Talc before veering sharply onto Guttergrow, which buttressed the back of Bal's hovel.

Jezebel followed. Unlike Jezebel in her simple green tunic, Shayla was dressed in an exquisite purple samite gown. A long, silver chain hung around her neck. She carried herself with an air of purpose that was difficult to place: when she passed someone in the street, they invariably gawked, struck by her station, only to look away a split second later, unnerved by the same ineffable quality that gave the Long-Eyes her power. Shayla might have been a priestess or a slum lord, a highborn lady or a whore.

Jezebel followed in her wake, unseen.

They arrived at The Spider Hole. It was a squat and dingy abode, sandwiched between ramshackle buildings. Although it was early, a handful of patrons were already quaffing ale, in early celebration of Queen Portia's arrival. Jezebel followed Shayla across the sawdust-covered floor, toward a mustachioed man on the opposite side of the room. While crossing, Jezebel glanced at the cupboard where the dragonfeeder purportedly had slept when she was a poor orphan girl. The man opened a door in the dusky black that spilled back out into the day, revealing a cramped courtyard full of empty wooden benches. Standing in the middle of the courtyard was a man with a long beard tied into sections by pieces of colored string. He stood awaiting them, holding his hands behind his back, striking a subservient air.

"Madam Shayla," the man intoned. He didn't so much as glance at Jezebel.

Shayla gave the man a generous smile. "Jezebel, this is Jodori Flak, from the Blackstar Isles. He is a man of many, shall we say, unnatural talents. I've brought him here today to teach you one. The ability to breathe fire."

Jezebel blanched. It was only then that she noticed the torch lying on the ground beside Jodori, latent with igneous potential. "Breathe fire?" she repeated.

"Yes. When you emerge on Teriquay's back tomorrow night, you will breathe real fire, for the delight of our queen."

A pang of fear and a thrill of excitement passed through Jezebel simultaneously. The words *at last* materialized in her mind as a different sentiment escaped her lips.

"Is it...safe?"

Shayla laughed, a throaty chuckle. "I should hope not. Not entirely, at least. If the queen and her court aren't for a heartbeat's breadth distressed, then it won't have had the desired effect. You'll be in some danger too, of course, but that's why Jodori's here. To guide you on the path between entertainment and immolation."

The Blackstar Islander nodded with a curt fervency. He turned to Jezebel without looking at her, his sightline skewing high. "Fire is an unpredictable beast, but she can be directed, corralled. I'll teach you secrets enough to see you safely through your performance."

Jezebel found herself nodding, agreeing. Even so, another question formed. "Theus, Trudy, and Roger—are they aware? I suppose we'll need to practice at least once onstage, later tonight, for their benefit."

Shayla's response was studied, calm. "No. They're to be kept in the dark. The first knowledge that they'll have of the fire will be the moment you breathe Teriquay's flames over the tops of their heads." She paused. Smiled her cat's-grin smile. "The moment will be sublime. Beautiful. Performance will blur into reality, and for an instant both the audience and the Queen of Ragar Or will exist in the same suspended space that held King Reuel and his family before Teriquay's flames ushered them into oblivion."

Jezebel unconsciously held her breath. In her mind's eye she was atop the wooden Teriquay, watching the flame billow over the heads of the imitation Salks, hearing the astonished and frightened cries from both the actors onstage and the crowd beyond. Jezebel had played the part of the dragonfeeder for so long that it felt as if the girl were a part of her very being; here was an opportunity to tap even deeper into the experience, to go beyond becoming the role and elicit, at the crucial moment, the same primal fear the dragonfeeder had once demanded from those caught beneath the dragon's flame.

"I'll do it," Jezebel said.

*

They practiced with watered wine. Jodori showed Jezebel how to pocket the liquid at the front of her mouth, how to close off the back of her throat. Then, over and over again, Jodori bid her spew the wine into the air toward an imaginary torch held at a sixty-degree angle, forcefully and tight-lipped with a raspberry pucker and "harder, harder!" Once or twice droplets of spewed wine landed on Jezebel's chin, causing Jodori to shake his head and lament the envisioned loss of her beautiful face. "Now the fire has fallen, you see, and now your face is aflame, and now you are screaming, and now you are dead, or if alive, wishing it wasn't so." Then he would demonstrate once more, and afterwards have her grab hold of his bone-dry beard, upon which no droplets of wine had fallen.

At last, Jodori stepped away from Jezebel and declaimed, "It is time." He reached into the pocket of his green-and-black cloak and retrieved a leather-skin pouch. "Lamp oil," he said. "More effective than watered wine." He sighed, seemingly apropos of nothing, before going to work on the torch. Within minutes he had the torch lit, striking iron onto flint near the torch's pine-pitch/cedar bark head. "Tomorrow Shayla will provide the torch. It will be lit for you." Jezebel had lit a torch before, but she nodded in agreement, knowing that during the madness of the play, stopping to light a torch would be next to impossible.

Once again Jodori retrieved the leather pouch. Moving to a clearing in the middle of the courtyard, he took a pull from the pouch, lifted the blazing torch into the air, and, in quick succession, spewed three short blasts, bringing a trio of fireballs into existence. The heat from the fireballs warmed Jezebel's face. She felt a sort of giddiness overcome her at the thought of bringing the element into being.

"Now, you," he said, handing over the torch. The flame danced at the torch's end like a restless spirit, awaiting the instruction of her breath. Once the torch was secure in Jezebel's hand, Jodori handed over the leather-skin pouch. Her heartbeat thrummed in and out of time to the flickering flame. Before she could reconsider, she pocketed a mouthful of oil, gathered her strength, and, copying Jodori, spewed thrice. A flower of flame bloomed each time, its dangerous orange blossoms crowning the empty air. When she had finished, the flame resettled on the head of the torch, still dancing, still agitated.

Jezebel turned to Jodori and smiled. A drop of lamp oil trembled on her lip, pining for the flame.

*

She trailed the royal procession back to the Three Dragons Inn. The common folk were peeling away in Jezebel's wake, tears of joy in many an eye. It seemed everyone had seen the queen, who, from the sound of it, had presented a magnificent figure: from snippets of conversation Jezebel heard the queen described as a "golden butterfly," "Stavus's own daughter," "right pretty for an old 'un," "the Twin Ascendant, no doubt," and, from a man who seemed intent on the Ontish angle, "the very picture of a Salk, Beoliotius guide her, with her high hard cheekbones and jaw. The Twins had good sense to cut down that Sparrot fellow in his prime and give our dynasty to Ontish blood."

At the foot of the hill leading up to the Three Dragons, a group of mounted knights had formed a soft perimeter. They looked a magnificently fierce lot, resplendent in surcoats bearing the Salk insignia: three crows perched on a tree limb against a field of beige. In their midst, a familiar face. One of the stagehands—a torchbearer named Ewe—sat puffed up and prideful on the back of a tan rouncy, looking for all the world like the keeper of the realm. When he saw Jezebel, a self-important expression took hold of his face.

"This, gents," he began, turning to the knights, "is why our Lady of the Long-Eyes…meaning Madam Shayla…asked me to stand post. The lovely lass you see before you is no common village wench come to beggar the queen's time. No, she is Jezebel, the dragonfeeder, the very one the fortunate few will have the honor of watching perform on the morrow. Her residence is the Three Dragons, her home the stage. Unlike the others, she passes."

"Stavus save us," a different knight said, rolling his eyes. But upon taking their measure of Jezebel, the other knights collectively decided that they didn't mind. One of the younger knights leaned forward in the saddle. "You play the part of the dragonfeeder? Truly?"

"Yes," Jezebel replied, keeping her expression distant, neutral. She knew a million ways to keep men at bay, polite detachedness being the first arrow in her quiver.

"Don't the legends say the dragonfeeder was a scrawny thing? You, you're so…"

"Womanly," a russet-bearded knight finished on his behalf. He wore a grin like an eel for Jezebel's benefit, before quickly redirecting his attention to the younger knight. "It's a performance, you fig-eater. You don't ask the nobility to hand over a brogan's-head and then trot out a teatless scarecrow to perform. You've got to keep their attention." He turned back to Jezebel with the same soulless smile and made a presentation of her with his hands.

She replicated the smile and the gesture. "May I pass?" She felt a tickle in her throat, a sort of hot burning. After fire-breathing with Jodori, she had washed out the lamp oil with a strong ale, but now the taste of the lamp oil returned in force. She briefly envisioned roaring flame at the men, striding through the charred remains. She glanced past the knights to the top of the hill where the Three Dragons awaited—both the inn and the sculpted trio atop the inn. Teriquay's open jaw stretched toward the unwitting knights, its exposed gullet yearning to feast or, perhaps, preparing to flame.

A strange and wary look suddenly came over the face of the russet-bearded knight. Without saying a word, he gave Jezebel a little nod, reined back his horse, and receded to the left. The knights to the right and left of him respectively did the same, creating a part in the perimeter.

Jezebel passed, continuing to the inn.

*

When she walked inside, a woman who could have only been Queen Portia was descending the spiral staircase, accompanied by the royal retainer. The queen paused her descent when Jezebel entered. Mimicking their liege, Queen Portia's retainers did the same, until, in very short fashion, every person in sight was staring at Jezebel.

Jezebel couldn't help but return the queen's gaze. Her Highness was an arresting woman, even in her old age. The queen's hair was a black storm cloud streaked with lightning strikes of silver-grey, the legendary Salk mane. It framed an intelligent, venerable face that possessed notes of kindness and authority. She was slightly shorter than average height, a fact that in no way undercut her palpably evident charisma. She was clad in the sumptuary fashion, wearing a silver surcoat embroidered with the regalia of her house. The Salk family crest, its colors altered for the season, danced on the fabric, looking stylized and less formal than expected, though certainly not less expensive. *She's Beoliotius in the flesh,* Jezebel thought passingly. *The mother of the Twins.*

"Madam Shayla," the queen intoned, her voice sounding like honey poured over volcanic rock, "would you do us the honor of introducing our new guest?"

It was only then that Jezebel noticed Shayla Long-Eyes. She was standing on the steps beneath the queen, surprisingly inconspicuous. There were no obvious differences—her hair and dress remained the same—but she seemed to have retreated into herself somehow, and, in doing so, become a different person. Shayla gave the queen a quick smile in response, but it was the smile of the meek and the mild, devoid of the hunger and power that generally characterized her every facial expression.

When Shayla Long-Eyes spoke, her voice sounded like a trembling creek of water. "My Queen. Before you stands the young lady of whom I spoke: Jezebel White, the actress who plays the dragonfeeder."

The expression on Queen Portia's face suggested she had guessed as much. "Jezebel," the queen said, letting the name sit unadorned in the space of a restive silence. Jezebel, to break the unease of simply standing there, gave a deep curtsy, and hung her head. Head bowed, she heard what sounded like the queen harrumphing. "Oh please, child, do raise your head." Jezebel ended her curtsy, and once more found the queen's eyes. "You will sup with me tonight, will you not?" the queen asked, though of course it wasn't really a question.

"Yes, Your Highness," Jezebel replied.

"Good," the queen said. Her expression had changed once more: she wore a grin that was full of either impish mischief or masked malice, it was difficult to say which. "As you can imagine, I have quite a few questions for the actress who spends her days killing my brother."

*

The Three Dragons Inn had a large common hall in the west wing, and that was where they dined. Over the years, Shayla had spared no expense in renovating the inn for the purpose of attracting ever-more affluent clientele; in no place was this more evident than the dining hall. Dying sunlight filtered through a series of gorgeous stained-glass windows on the hall's western wall. The three windows bore depictions of scenes from the play, one for each act, beginning with the dragonfeeder's ascension up the mountain and culminating with the dragon Teriquay's descent from the same, beautifully captured in a myriad of colors— green, gold, and white being dominant. On the southern wall hung a massive tapestry, showcasing the beauty of Low Osgood as seen from the perspective of someone standing at the front door of the Three Dragons Inn. The Long-Eyes had commissioned the work from a master weaver out of Wrain, an eccentric artist named Cipriot who had spent time in Clyesia learning the art of perspective. Jezebel often stared in wonder at the work. Looking at the tapestry, she felt as if she might step into the fabric and begin the winding walk away from the inn, down toward the glistening perfection of Lake Wyglass in the distance.

An extravagant dinner was served. The queen's own traveling cook had prepared the fare, and he had made it a point to prepare plates that blended the south with the north, the Struvan with the Ontish, the rivers and seas with the land and sky. A cherry and corn salad preceded a spice-dusted mountain river trout. Soon after, roasted heartbirds served in black-bread trenches arrived, followed by a sweet stew made from Qorlish grasses. For the main course, a hearty moonbear dish was served, the meat glistening red and served with a savory brown sauce. The queen in particular was enamored with the plate.

"When I was a child, Father would tell my brother and I stories of how grandfather stayed alive during the Crow and Arrow Rebellion by eating moonbear. Usually the moonbear was dried and salted, but once, when he was in his cups, Father scared Reuel and I to death by telling us a story of how Grandfather stalked and slew a moonbear to stave off starvation. I can't remember what was more frightening—hearing how the moonbear nearly decapitated Grandfather with a swipe of its massive paw or listening to how Grandfather cut out the moonbear's liver and ate it raw seconds after the bear was dead."

Jezebel, seated next to the queen, nodded dumbly, uncertain how to respond. Multiple people were listening in, but the queen's attention was directed at Jezebel. A few responses rattled around Jezebel's skull, but they were too stupid to share: *Your grandfather was Daeguss Salk, the first king of Ragar Or, your father was King Brogan I, and your brother Reuel was burnt to a crisp by the dragon Teriquay.* Jezebel kept hoping that Shayla, seated opposite and on the other side of the queen, would jut into the conversation, but the Long-Eyes appeared committed to her newfound meekness.

"Your grandfather must have been a brave and fierce man, Your Highness," Jezebel managed at last.

The queen bent an eyebrow at Jezebel and gave a small smile. "All the legends say so," she replied. "And now that my grandfather is a legend, he will remain forever thus. Personally, I'm partial to stories of Grandfather's kingship, when he became known as Daeguss the Unifier." The queen looked distracted for a moment, before recovering. "But enough about my family. What I would really like to hear about is you. Did you know that I can scarce keep company at court for news of yet another noble going on holiday to see *The Flame*? And when they return, all they can talk about is the hypnotic performance of the girl who plays the dragonfeeder. But now I'm the one in Low Osgood, and I mean to drink my fill of the experience. So tell me—how did you come to play the part?"

Jezebel had a sense of the dangers inherent to conversing with royalty, but, seeing that the die had been cast, she summoned her thespian nerve and committed to the moment. "I had no acting experience before winning the role, Your Highness. When I first came to Low Osgood, I saw a troupe perform *Arrival of the Ships* by the lake. It was the first play that I had ever seen, and it stirred my soul in unexpected ways. It seemed to me that the actors had not merely performed a play—they had carved out a different reality for themselves, and there made a home. I was desperate to live in that space, if only for the span of a couple of hours each day. Months later, word spread around Low Osgood that there was to be an open audition for an ongoing play to be held at the new inn on Simstone. I gathered my courage and came."

"And you won the part, without any prior acting experience?"

"Yes, Your Highness." She was uncertain to what degree she should elaborate. "Madam Shayla chose me."

The collective weight of the queen's attention shifted to Shayla Long-Eyes. Shayla donned a demure smile. Her voice when she responded sounded like a light rain. "Jezebel was the correct choice for the dragonfeeder. Any simpleton would have recognized it."

The queen's curiosity wasn't so easily allayed. "And yet you were the one who *did* recognize it." The queen smiled yet again, a paring-knife grin. "We searched for the dragonfeeder for years, you know. We searched for the dragon too. All three dragons, in fact. They went wild after Reuel's death: Mooncalf and Comet set fire to a nearby village before disappearing. Few remember those details. But everyone remembers the dragonfeeder. Don't they?"

Jezebel's heart gave a little tremble. Was the question intended for her? The space of the silence that followed was unbearable; Jezebel felt an urgent need to say anything that would bring the quiet to an end.

"The dragonfeeder was evil, Your Highness. Evil is memorable. But the dragonfeeder's story is compelling only because it's balanced by the story of the Salk dynasty, who weren't undone by the tragedy of Reuel's death. At the end of the play..." Jezebel halted, worried that she might soil the queen's experience of the play on the morrow.

Queen Portia laughed. "Continue, my child. I may not have seen the play, but every scene has been described for me a hundred times over."

Jezebel continued. "At the end of the play, the actress who plays Your Highness comes onstage and delivers an impassioned monologue mourning the death of her brother and her brother's family. She then promises that the Salk line will continue through her, and that the realm will not be destroyed by so senseless and vile an act. It's the queen's words that make the play redemptive. Her goodness—the Salks' goodness—is what gives the audience permission to be fascinated by the dragonfeeder. I've played the role of the dragonfeeder for years, and never once has the audience applauded when I've set foot onstage. But for your brother, for you...they cheer and clap, or they cry, because of their love for the Salks. Their love for Ragar Or."

"They clap for you at the end, do they not? When you return to the stage and take your bow?"

Jezebel flushed with a sudden guilt. It was true that no one clapped for her during the play, but, at the end, her cheers were always the loudest. "Y...Yes, You...Your Highness," she stuttered.

The table had grown deathly quiet. Only six were seated at the head table; down below in the benches, the burbling of conversation continued unabated, lively and good-natured.

"Make no mistake about the audience, dear girl," the queen said, her voice growing dark. "They clap and cheer because they are entertained." The queen's onyx eyes zeroed in on Jezebel. "That's a lesson we queens and kings know best of all. In order to rule, one must put on a good show."

*

Jezebel's dreams that night were wild, unstable things. She struggled to find solid footing in her subconscious, as the dreamscape kept changing from moment to moment. One moment she was a child back in Coffyn Castle, searching in the shadows of the keep for the lost members of her family, and the next she was a ball of flame, bright and powerful, filled with her own potency. The twin sister she had scarcely known appeared again and again, but at the very moment Jezebel became cognizant of her sister's identity, the child or the woman would vanish into nothingness. Later, Jezebel was onstage at the amphitheater, weeping for her lost sibling to an audience enthralled. The emotion was so powerful that she dropped to her knees in anguish. A fellow actress brought her to her feet. When Jezebel wiped away her tears, she saw that it was Shayla Long-Eyes, staring at her with whorled blue eyes, communicating a secret message. Behind the curtain, the dragons were coming to life, but, try as she might, Jezebel couldn't look away from Shayla. The sound of beating wings and the screams from the audience and the smell of smoke and the sense that all would soon be enveloped in flame mattered not: she was trapped in Shayla's gaze, unable to flee, unable to wake, and she knew that soon it would be too late...

She awoke to the sound of a rapping on the door. Outside, daybreak was worming free from the clutches of night. Crossing the room, Jezebel had the distinct sensation that she had not left the world of dreams entirely behind. When she opened the door, Queen Portia was standing there. The queen was flanked by the knight with the russet beard. Behind the queen and the knight stood Shayla, tallow candle in hand, head bowed meekly toward the floor.

Jezebel felt a sudden surge of anger and embarrassment. She was dressed in a simple chemise slip, and the russet-bearded knight made no effort to hide the fact that his eyes were drinking their fill. She nearly said something cross, but a small voice in the back of her mind reminded her whose man she was addressing. She steadied herself. "Good morning, Your Highness," she said, and gave a small curtsy.

Queen Portia didn't reply. She simply stood there, studying Jezebel with a firm, expressionless face. The splendid silver surcoat from the day before was gone; now the queen wore stately black samite offset by a cream-colored collar and sash. Around her neck, a silver chain strained against the weight of a dazzling red ruby.

As the silence grew, so did Jezebel's fear. She lowered her gaze and took slow, deep breaths, trying to calm her rapidly accelerating heart.

At last, the queen gathered her dress. "Step back, child," she commanded. Jezebel gave way, and the queen entered the room. Shayla Long-Eyes and the bearded knight followed.

Once inside, Queen Portia drew herself up in all her imperious might, wearing an authoritative expression that bespoke the power of her station. The Salk Queen hadn't come for niceties. That much was clear.

"Take off your clothes," the queen ordered.

Jezebel blanched. "Why?"

"Because I command it."

Jezebel's lips parted, but instead of summoning a reason for refusal, she was struck dumb by the sudden understanding of why the queen wanted her naked. *She thinks I'm a jeyedoshi. She wants to see if I have the telling mark.* She glanced at the others. The knight was too busy devouring her with his hungry eyes to meet her own. Shayla, however, held Jezebel in a soft and steady gaze, imparting an unexpected strength. Jezebel drew from Shayla's power like a plant feeding on the sun.

Jezebel faced the queen. She pulled the slip over the top of her head and let it fall to the floor, exposing her form in all its glory.

Queen Portia inspected her carefully. She swept Jezebel's long, dark-blonde mane from the nape of Jezebel's neck so that her eyes could climb the stepladder of Jezebel's spine to the base of Jezebel's skull. She roamed the shapely plains of Jezebel's body with a meticulous thoroughness, studying first the front and then the back, making pass after pass after endless pass. A deep quiet set in, the only sound the occasional request from the queen for Jezebel to turn this way or that. For the longest time the queen looked at Jezebel without touching her. But then, when it seemed that all was nearly concluded, the queen lifted Jezebel's arms and studied underneath; and then she did the same to Jezebel's breasts; and then she searched ever more intimate areas of Jezebel's body, adjusting Jezebel's position as she saw fit.

Jezebel bore it all in silence. Behind her, the rising sun suffused the room with an orange-purple glow, bruised from its daily battle with Simstone Mountain. The amphitheater was just outside the window. Jezebel thought of the adolescents who had fought there years ago, the multitude who had died. Twins, they called them, though Jezebel knew that most of those who fought weren't real twins; the Ontish would pair children with similar physical characteristics together, and then, after a year-long period in which the children trained and lived and ate together, the pair would fight to the death. All this was done in honor of Daeguss and Ropske, the twins the Ontish believed founded Ragar Or thousands of years ago. Daeguss's tribe—the Onts—survived: he was ever after known as the Twin Ascendant. *I had a real twin once,* Jezebel thought. *Her name was Lilia. She smelled of fresh straw and honeysuckle. She fell down a well and died when she was three years old. My mother flung herself down the same well in her grief.*

Queen Portia finished her inspection. She turned to address Shayla. "It's as you said. She has no telling mark."

Jezebel floated back into her body. The wolfish knight was still leering at her. Surprising even herself, Jezebel hissed at him. Her hissing made the knight flush beneath his beard, the red bramble growing redder still.

The queen suddenly remembered the knight. "Oh, do get out, Sir Dougal," the queen said. The knight, embarrassed, turned on his heel and left.

Jezebel faced the queen. She felt wild. She readied another hiss on her tongue, but, before she could loose it, she sensed Shayla warning her off. Jezebel assented, though her thoughts remained a blank rage.

The queen addressed Jezebel. "Thirty-one years ago, my brother came to Low Osgood the King of all Ragar Or. A jeyedoshi sent him to his death. You will understand if I take every precaution to ensure that I don't suffer the same fate."

Jezebel's thoughts lurched back into being. *I had a twin sister, but I am no jeyedoshi. Every member of my family died, but I am no jeyedoshi. I play the part of a jeyedoshi, but I am no jeyedoshi. I have no telling mark. I do not speak to animals. And I know no dragon that I might summon from the heavens to roast you to death.* But to the queen she replied, "I understand, Your Highness."

The queen said nothing. She seemed to realize that the currency of words had little value in the aftermath of what had occurred.

All at once the Salk monarch grew uncomfortable with Jezebel's continued nudity. She looked away from Jezebel, and turned to Shayla. "Consider me convinced, Madam Shayla. It is clear that your play is meant to edify—and not corrupt—the realm. I hope that my…precautions…will in no way detract from the performance that I have waited so long to see."

Shayla responded to the half-request, half-command with a gracious smile. "Of course not, Your Highness. The players will give their queen the performance of a lifetime. Of that I can assure you."

The queen gave a little nod. "Good." Her salted black mane shifted in the direction of Jezebel, but, before turning all the way, she caught herself, and stopped. Then, without saying another word, she exited the room.

*

Jezebel retreated to a pinewood chest on the opposite side of the room and selected her clothing for the day. With the queen gone, she felt more numb than ashamed. Shayla remained in the room while she dressed. When Jezebel was at last clothed, she turned and faced Shayla. The Long-Eyes had a question waiting on her tongue.

"Do you know the Four Prayers of the Twins?" Shayla Long-Eyes asked.

It wasn't a question that Jezebel had expected. When Jezebel was a girl, the Twins had held sway at Coffyn Castle. Adulthood had brought Jezebel in contact with many and more who worshipped Stavus, the Struvan deity of light and air, but Jezebel's earliest memories were of Lord Wexel Coffyn and Lady Esme Coffyn standing under an immense night sky, asking Beoliotius—the mother of the Twins—to bless them with wealth.

"I remember the prayer for wealth."

Shayla smiled, her lips blooming like the petals of a crimson flower. She seemed to be expanding now that the queen was no longer in the room. Her voluminous hair shook free from unseen strictures, her buxom body relaxed into space, and her eyes, ever rapacious, roamed the room unchecked, preying on whatever they desired.

"You only heard the Lord and Lady Coffyn recite the prayer, am I right? Never your mother and father."

Jezebel nodded. She knew what Shayla was referencing. Only lords and ladies were permitted to recite the prayer for wealth. If a commoner was caught reciting it, they'd be whipped.

"Do you know any of the other prayers?"

"The prayer for health." It was the one prayer Jezebel had carried with her into adulthood, the one she knew by heart. She whispered it every now and then to the night sky, not because she believed that it would work, but because she thought that doing so couldn't hurt.

"The prayer for health is the most common prayer. Even those who worship Stavus say it. Its overuse has made it an empty prayer, devoid of meaning. Prayers only have power when they are used sparingly."

Jezebel could see the truth in that. She reflected on the hundreds of times she'd mouthed the prayer for health in thoughtless fear, hoping to ward off sickness. If it had any effect, it seemed more a matter of coincidence than divine intervention.

"And the last two?" Shayla asked.

Jezebel racked her brain, but nothing came to her. She wasn't a religious person. The Twins were the gods of the gorgostrine, the gods of the peninsulas, the gods of high northern lords, the gods of long ago. She had seen a gorgostrine once, preaching by the waterfront, but no prayers had fallen from his lips. Perhaps she had once known the other two prayers, but, if so, that was the case no longer.

Jezebel shook her head.

A strange life force flooded Shayla's face. "The prayer for death. And the prayer for vengeance."

A deep and palpable silence entered the room like a guest of honor. Jezebel and Shayla wordlessly agreed to give the silence its say. *The prayer for death. And the prayer for vengeance.* The names of the two prayers hovered in the secret spaces of Jezebel's mind like summoned ghosts. Near the spirits, a shadow memory. Jezebel's father, standing beneath a bowl of stars, crying, dark and earnest words trembling on his lips.

Shayla stood across from Jezebel, seeing all.

This isn't for you, Jezebel warned.

"We were both little girls once," Shayla said, ending the quiet.

The silence again, more familiar this time. It wore a cloak of suggestion, then laughed when Jezebel guessed correctly.

"The queen came to my room first," Shayla continued. "The same knight stripped me roughly bare, then stood to the side to see that I followed orders. The queen studied my naked body twice as long as she studied yours. And me a woman past my prime. But her words were sufficiently honeyed that I knew she was only frightened and taking precautions. She looked in my eyes at the last. She saw nothing but a peaceful ocean of blue."

The reoccurring hush.

The queen saw what you wanted her to see, Jezebel thought.

"They say the dragonfeeder recited the prayer as she descended from the heavens to smite King Reuel. You are not a Jeyedoshi," Shayla said. "But even a non-Jeyedoshi can recite the prayer for vengeance to great effect. Listen. I'll teach it to you.

> *Whole, we shall be cleaved*
> *And ever after strive against our whole selves*
> *For who is the other now but an imposter*
> *Deserving only of death*
> *Mother Beoliotius*
> *Daeguss, Ropske*
> *Grant me vengeance*
> *Against my friends, my siblings, my enemies."*

Jezebel heard the prayer only once, but it was sufficient to commit it to memory. She said the words over and over again in her mind.

She was still saying the prayer when Shayla Long-Eyes left the room.

*

The play began later than usual.

The players performed in front of a packed amphitheater nearly every night, but the ceremony involved in seating Queen Portia's court delayed the start by nearly thirty minutes. Word spread backstage of the wonder of the benches: the Salk banner flew from twelve staffs staked into the ground around the seating area, smaller-scale complements to the large Salk standard now flying from atop the Three Dragons Inn. The flag on top of the inn was so large that it obscured the sculpture of the three dragons.

"Crows, crows, and more crows," Osten detailed to the others after sneaking a peek at the flags moments before the opening curtain. "I wouldn't be surprised if midway through the opening act the benches take flight and we're made to perform the remainder of the play flying above Wyglass. Personally, it would be a nice change of pace. Fond as I am of Comet, his use of wheels rather than wings leaves me perpetually disappointed."

Only a few laughed. The tensions were too high. Some of the players were so stressed that they diverged from their pre-performance routines. Theus, known for nipping a potent black rum before taking the stage, gulped from the flask. Angiel, who liked to sing bawdy songs, hummed a Stavusian hymn. Meric, a talker, meditated. Roger, the boy who played Prince Daeguss, eschewed his normal gallivanting and sat quietly in a corner.

It took Jezebel to dispel the tension. When the curtain parted, she took to the stage and delivered an opening monologue of spellbinding intensity, juxtaposing the daily trials of the dragonfeeder's orphaned existence with a passionate, disquieting desire to scale the heights of nearby Mount Tribune and master the dragon Teriquay. The queen and the queen's court sat entranced. The dragonfeeder was no easy heroine, no easy villain. She was a wounded, courageous, and angry girl, a girl who had an inkling of her jeyedoshi nature and had resolved to harness it to full effect, damn the consequences.

The other players rallied after Jezebel's opening speech. When the play segued into court life, the actors and actresses playing Salk royalty infused their performances with a transcendental energy. The play soon took on a life of its own, as both the crowd and the actors were swept along on an alternate tide of time. Hours, days, and months passed onstage, in neat rhythm to the timeless performance devouring the here and now.

Jezebel gave herself over to the performance most of all. The events of the previous few days were not forgotten so much as fed like kindling into the fire of her art. She had long learned how to forget herself whenever she performed, but tonight the dragonfeeder's essence seemed to burn in her very skin. She thought perhaps there would be no need of the torch awaiting her at the play's end; the flame was already in her throat.

She walked offstage after the dragonfeeder's penultimate scene in the same headspace. She slipped into the diaphanous lace slip, feeling like she was the dragonfeeder incarnate. She said naught as the makeup artist transformed the whorl on her cheek from faint sky to a vibrant blue. She strode to the wooden emerald-green dragon like it was her birthright, and she climbed the steps like she was mounting Teriquay's own back.

It wasn't until the stagehand appeared with the torch that Jezebel startled from the role. Ewe—the stagehand who had vouched for her in front of the queen's knights the day before—emerged from the shadows holding the flame. "My lady," he said with a strained grace. He looked at the floor with a subservient gaze, and handed over the torch.

Jezebel accepted the torch from Ewe with her right hand. She held a leather pouch filled with lamp oil in her left hand. It had been waiting on Teriquay's top step, just as Shayla Long-Eyes had said it would. Jezebel swept the flame back and forth, taking in the other backstage actors, who looked at her with confused expressions. She waited for the inevitable question, the witty remark, the humorous quip. Instead, everyone held their tongues. After a moment, Jezebel felt compelled to explain.

"A surprise," she said. "For the finale."

Meric, Theon and Osten gave uneasy nods, but none spoke. Ewe piped up instead. "I must leave, my lady. We torchbearers have a part to play as well."

He sprinted away.

The muffled voices of King Reuel and his doomed family conversed on the opposite side of the curtain. It was time for Jezebel to lean forward and wrap her hands around the dragon's neck, but, with the torch and lamp oil in hand, she found it impossible. *Should I pocket the lamp oil in my cheeks now?* Her thoughts, a rushing stream all night, became a slurry.

She thumbed open the leather pouch and tipped the lamp oil into her mouth.

The side curtains opened. The sight of Comet and Mooncalf provoked the usual response from the crowd, a chorus of oohs and aahs. Flustered and running short of time, Jezebel futilely tried to thumb the leather pouch back closed. Failing, she gave up and dropped the pouch on Teriquay's top step, where the oil slicked around her feet. *I cannot reach the grips,* she thought. Theon read her mind. "We'll go slowly, my lady. Focus on staying upright."

Onstage, King Reuel gave his cue. "They are a pair, which means they are blessed by the Twins, and they are creatures of the air, which delights Stavus. The gods shine on these creatures, just as the gods shine on all of

Ragar Or." The center curtain parted. The audience vocalized their wonder at the sight of Teriquay, their fright. For the first time all night, Jezebel broke from her role long enough to actually look at the crowd. The queen was sitting front center. Jezebel caught the queen's eyes, and for a second they beheld each other in the raw power of the moment.

She forced herself to look away from Queen Portia as the stagehands rolled her slowly toward the boat. *It's darker than usual,* Jezebel thought. The play was timed to end near sunset, but, because of the late start, twilight had fallen. Jezebel's eyes continued to roam. Through the gauze of torch smoke, Jezebel cast her gaze at the heavens, and caught a glimpse of the sentinel stars. To the north, the moonbear's eyes preceded its face, while high above and slightly behind Jezebel, the Jailer looked down from his vigilant perch.

Giving up the skies, Jezebel's attention was drawn to the corners of the amphitheater, where, to her surprise, the black-clothed torchbearers had congregated. She watched with surprise as the boy who had delivered her torch now took a different flame and walked with the others down the aisles on the outside of the benches. Soon every row was lined by black-clothed torchbearers. The audience was enclosed: the Three Dragons Inn hemmed in the queen's court from behind, the torchbearers guarded the aisles, and the stage and Simstone blocked the front.

Why are they there? They're not supposed to—

"Father, look." Roger, the boy who played Prince Daeguss, was fighting through the many distractions to deliver his lines. His voice was laced with unease; he couldn't take his eyes off Jezebel's torch. "It's the green dragon. The wild one."

Jezebel noted that a handful of the audience had taken note of the torchbearers, but, for the most part, the queen and her court kept their attentions fixed on the stage. *They've no reason to think that what's happening isn't a normal part of the play.* In her distraction, Jezebel nearly forgot to keep her throat closed. Lamp oil slid toward her esophagus, but Jezebel kept from swallowing.

There was movement at the back of the amphitheater. A man with a tied-off beard slipped inside the Three Dragons Inn.

King Reuel hesitated with his lines. He looked as if he desperately wanted to ask Jezebel a question. "Teriquay," he said at last. His voice, always affected with disquiet, was even more so. "She's wild, yes, but as harmless as the other two." The king offered the prince a protective, paternal arm. "She must have sensed that we were here. She's come to pay homage."

The prayer. I'm supposed to say the prayer for vengeance. The same as the dragonfeeder did when she descended from the sky. The words came quickly to mind, but, with her mouth full of lamp oil, Jezebel could only recite the prayer as a thought. Unlike when she said the prayer this morning, the words felt false, as if they belonged to someone else.

Whose vengeance is this?

"Reuel. Look! Teriquay has a rider. Why does she have a rider?"

The play's great hush descended. Jezebel prepared for the brisk push, bracing her feet as best as she could against the slick of the lamp oil. But Theon, sensing Jezebel's unsteadiness, chose to push the dragon forward slowly. The actors in the boat, thrown by the change in Teriquay's pace, neither shrieked nor shielded their faces.

Jezebel froze. She had forgotten who she was. Her eyes flitted to the inn. She thought she saw a flame licking at one of the windows. *It's only a trick of the torches,* she told herself. She looked back at the audience, desperately trying to find the courage to breathe fire into the air. Every eye was upon her, including those of the torchbearers, who appeared to be waiting for a cue. *I am the dragonfeeder,* she told herself. *I am Jezebel. I am the dragonfeeder and I am Jezebel. There is no line between performance and reality.* But still, she did nothing.

Then Jezebel saw her. Shayla Long-Eyes. She had been sitting at the back of the benches, but now she was standing, staring straight at the stage. Staring straight at Jezebel. She smiled in that confident way of hers, as if the future was already written.

Maybe it is, Jezebel thought. *Maybe it's been predestined all along.*

Shayla kept staring at Jezebel, refusing to look away. Jezebel acquiesced to the Long-Eyes's power. She knew without a doubt who Shayla was, and she knew what Shayla wanted from her.

Shayla raised an imaginary torch into the air and breathed an invisible fire.

Jezebel forgot her fears and collapsed back into the moment. She raised the torch into the air and gave life to the flame, causing the fiery petals to blossom once, twice, three times. They expanded with each iteration, until, on the last, the fire transformed into something more, something larger, a being that, once unleashed, could not be controlled. *How?* Jezebel wondered, but she laughed even as she wondered, a painful screaming laugh soon to be echoed by hundreds of others. The world turned to orange and white. Jezebel, flailing, searched for the black, the night sky where it was said the Twins answered prayers. But all her desperate eyes could find was a great dragon descending, beating its blazing wings, heeding her call.

THANKS FOR READING

If you enjoyed *Last Performance at the Three Dragons Inn,* please consider leaving a review on Amazon and/or Goodreads to help spread the word.

To receive the latest news about *The Song of the Burning Heart* series, please sign up for my newsletter at benspencer.substack.com.

I hope that you will consider joining me on the journey to come.

www.ingramcontent.com/pod-product-compliance
Lightning Source LLC
Chambersburg PA
CBHW020319150626
46552CB00022B/2996